To my daughter, the light of my life.
No monster is too big when we fight side by side.
—AS

To my love, Aaron, who fights my fears.
—AB

My Monster Friends and Me

A Big Kid's Guide to Things That Go Bump in the Night

words by **Annie Sarac**

pictures by **Alice Brereton**

sourcebooks
wonderland

When I was your age, I knew where to hide,
for my house had many dark **monsters** inside.
Everywhere I looked, every corner and hall,
lurked creatures and beasts—furry, spiky, and tall!

I shook and I trembled. I huddled in fright.
I stared at the **darkness** till the wee morning light.
I bet you have monsters just as scary and gross.

Would you like to meet mine?
Come along—
but stay close!

I've got a secret I think you should hear
    about all these monsters and the **terrible fear**.
Now that I'm older—almost eight, you know—
    I'll share the truth that I learned long ago...

The first scary monster
    on the other side of that fence
made me shiver and cry
    and my muscles grow tense.

With its deep, snarly howl and sharp teeth and nails, it'd catch me one day with its

three slimy tails!

But as I got older, I learned a new trick.
If I **named** each monster,
the fear didn't stick.

That deep, loud barking,
the beast over that gate,

is just a darling
little terrier.

Monster One
is called
KATE!

Watch out for the **shadows**
and stay right by my side.
My second monster appears
as it gets dark outside.

Because right on my heels
and behind every chair
was a **spooky, dark monster**
with wild, tangled hair.

Those slinky, slippery shadows,
   and the one always at your feet,
could be a new friend to play with.
   Monster Two I named PETE!

But there were other monsters lurking
even scarier still.
Can you guess what they were?
Can you feel the **thrill?**

Monster Three was banging outside in the night.
It **rumbled** and **roared** a ferocious fright.

A **groan** and a **blast** and a **crack** and a **crash**—
it came through the window with a bright, blinding **flash!**

All that **banging** on your window
and the **rumbling, crackling** din
are just the clouds and raindrops dancing.

Monster Three
I named
LYNN!

In the dark of the house was a monster **SO** creepy—
with such strange, yellow eyes, I'd **never** feel sleepy.
Monster Four was in the closet or right behind that door,
and sometimes, I would hear it slithering on the floor!

All the gloom in the cellar
and the unknown in the dark
is just the blanket of night.

Monster Four
I named
CLARK!

But there was another one lurking even **scarier** still.
Can you guess what it was?
You know the drill!

This fifth one was **frightening**.

This fifth one was **mean**.

This hideous monster
was the **worst** that I've seen!

There were sharp, clawing sounds

COMING
FROM UNDER
THE BED!

That's right. You guessed it!

Monster Five I named TED!

But here is that **secret** I want you to know:
though all of these monsters seemed terrible foes,

when you're huddled with your pillow,
lean over and you'll see.

We all get scared of monsters—
    yes, even I did, that's true—
but now you have the secret
    that I've passed along to you.

So when your monsters call
    and you start to feel afraid,
remember this, and just **imagine**
    they're new **friends** that you've made.

Now go out there
and spread the news
of **FEARS**
turned into
FRIENDS.

Name that monster,
change that picture—
YOU choose how the story ends.

A Note to Parents and Other Caring Adults

As the editors at Wonderland, we wanted to create a monster book that was a little different from the monster books we all know and love. We know fears are a common struggle for young children. According to findings from leading psychologists and children's health magazines, most children struggle with *many* fears throughout adolescence. With that knowledge in mind, we wanted to create a book with multiple monsters and have each monster you find lurking in these pages represent what psychologists identify as some of the most common fears for children: mean animals, loud noises, shadows, thunderstorms, darkness, being alone, and what might be under the bed or in the closet.

It takes time to gradually overcome these fears as children grow older, but there is something adults can do to help. We all want our children to grow up happy and confident, and research now suggests that comforting and encouraging your children to slowly face their fears will help familiarize them with their "monsters" and desensitize the problem. Since children's wild imaginations can play a large role in forming fears, we thought there would also be an amazing opportunity for them to harness that same creativity for good—naming the monsters or reimagining them as something friendly and fun.

In creating our books, we hope to entertain and delight children everywhere with charming storytelling. Where we can, we try to go beyond the story to provide useful tools for you and your children to harness as they grow up and become the readers of tomorrow. Thank you for allowing us the privilege of contributing to your child's collection of books.